WISHES

A Short Story Collection

J.E. Spina

PUBLISHED BY J.E. SPINA

COPYRIGHT 2025
J.E. Spina

Londonderry, New Hampshire

COVER BY JOHN SPINA
Wishing well by Pixaby.com

ISBN (paperback) 979-8-9874646-7-0

Library of Congress Control
Number: 2025918950

of the publisher except for the use of brief quotations in a book review.

ACKNOWLEDGEMENTS

A very special thank you to my wonderful beta readers, Patricia Bradley, Michele Rolfe and John Spina for working tirelessly to read and review my work and for their helpful input. Their assistance is invaluable and appreciated.

Thank you to my husband, John, for the beautiful cover and for all the dinners he cooked that made it possible for me to write.

Thank you, Pixaby.com, for the lovely wishing well on the cover.

DEDICATION

To all who make wishes and hope they come true, I wish them well. May all their granted wishes far exceed their expectations.

PREFACE

Each of these stories imparts a theme related to wishes. They also have underlying messages about life, peace, safety from harm, sacrifice, kindness, and blessings.

Sometimes the things we wish for in life are not always what they seem. We have ups and downs but try to make the best of good times and bad. There are occasions when we make wishes without thinking.

Like the saying goes, 'Be careful what you wish for.' While other times, things work out for the better, much to our surprise.

This collection will make you think about the next time you make a wish.

Contents

THE HOMESTEAD

This was what the old couple always wished to have – a peaceful place to live out their lives in safety on a land they could call their own. They didn't expect this!

It was time to retire from their jobs. Calvin had been a postman for thirty-five years while Amelia worked as a RN in a hospital for thirty years.

They felt that they had earned their time to retire and wanted to find a home that was out in the country to get away from city life. They found the city to be congested and dirty.

The old couple remembered the days when people swept the sidewalks and streets in front of their apartments. Now there was graffiti everywhere and people tossed papers, cans and other trash into the gutters.

Calvin and Amelia also no longer felt safe walking the streets at night to go to a movie, shopping or out to dinner.

They had given up doing any of that now as they grew older and worried about being accosted and robbed of what little they had.

One day they made up their minds to find a place to live out their lives, what little there was left, in a safer and peaceful part of the country. That day they visited a realtor far from their present home to inquire about a home away from the hustle and bustle of the city.

The realtor was surprised when the old couple stepped into her office with their request. She didn't answer right away but just stared at them.

Calvin spoke up, "Excuse me, Miss, but did you hear me?"

"I'm sorry, sir. Yes, I heard you. Please take a seat and I'll see what we have to offer. You said you are looking for a home in the country? How many rooms do you need? Do you need a lot of land?"

Calvin exchanged inquisitive looks with Amelia at the woman's question. "I think we need something small, just for the two of us. We don't need a lot of land because we cannot do the maintenance any longer.

Amelia nodded in agreement.

"Hmm, I see. Okay. We do have a couple of places. One is a five-room house with a small barn. It has twenty acres of land that will not have to be maintained if you choose not to do that. It has been wild for a long time. You would just have to mow your front, back and side lawns."

"Okay, I can pay someone to take care of that for me," Calvin responded.

"What is the other place?" Amelia asked.

"Well, the other place is about the same size with five rooms but no barn. It does have a one-car garage on the property and more land – forty acres. It borders conservation land that you will not have to worry about."

"That sounds good. When can we see both properties?" Calvin asked.

"Well, I can take you there now. It's about a forty-minute drive. They are not far apart either. In fact, they are on the same plot of land both bordering the conversation land."

What the realtor neglected to tell them was these two houses each had a history of some strange things happening there. She feared these things might discourage the couple from purchasing one of the houses. One had a murder committed there while the other was said to be haunted.

"They sound peaceful," Amelia retorted.

"Yes, I guess they are. There aren't many houses near them. The closest house is ten miles away. You will not hear any noises except the chirping of birds and other animals nearby in the woods," the realtor added.

"Where are the stores?" Calvin inquired.

"They are about ten miles away from a small family-owned store. A pharmacy is also ten miles away. There is a small center with a variety of other local stores fifteen miles away. Will that be a problem?"

"No, I don't think so. I am a nurse and can take care of Calvin. He is healthy for an old guy," she giggled.

"Yes, she already does take good care of me," he smiled at her and winked.

We can stock up with what food we need and I can do some canning and freezing ahead of time. We don't eat a lot and don't need to shop for much," Amelia added.

"That's good to know," the realtor said, as she looked anything but certain that this couple could take care of themselves.

They arrived at the first place and went in to inspect the house. The area around the house was quite dense with trees and bushes infringing on the property.

Calvin took all this in and walked around the yard to see what flat land was available in case they wanted to plant some vegetables and flowers.

Amelia called out to him, "Calvin, come inside and see this place. It's small and needs some major touchups here and there."

Calvin nodded and went inside. He looked around and noticed the dust and clutter of old furniture that looked abandoned. He pushed the chairs into the table to get by and walked through the kitchen inspecting the stove and refrigerator that appeared to be almost as old as he and his wife. He peeked into the small living room and saw a scratched and worn coffee table, a lumpy-looking couch, and end tables with lamps that had fringe that hung low over the base of the lamps. There was one chair that had a missing cushion on it, not that he wanted to sit in it anyway. The bathroom was even worse with rusted fixtures, a stained tub and no shower in sight.

The bedroom was small with a double bed that had a dirty quilt and pillows piled high with a strange stain on them. He went in for a closer look.

The realtor let the couple walk around the house and inspect it on their own while she waited in the kitchen, too nervous to go any further. She could feel the cold emanating all around her.

Amelia came alongside her husband and looked closer at the stained pillows. She whispered, "What is that? Is it what I think it is?"

"Looks that way to me, Amelia. I don't think this place is for us. Besides, there is too much work to do to make it habitable."

"I agree, dear."

"Maybe we should look at the other place," he said to the realtor. "This is not for us."

"Okay, no problem. Let's go. It's close by at the other end of this conservation land."

Calvin spoke quietly to Amelia, "I don't like the feel of this place. I felt cold as soon as I entered the house. Did you feel it?"

"Yes, I thought it was just me. I am always cold anyway," Amelia said as she shivered.

"I didn't like the looks of the furniture and appliances. None of them looked usable."

"I agree, Calvin. That's okay. Let's look at the second place. Maybe that will be the one for us."

"Okay," Calvin nodded glumly.

When they arrived at the second place they looked around outside first. There was plenty of land around the house that would give them space to plant a garden or two. They smiled as they took it all in.

"So far so good, Calvin. The land here is flat for our garden and I can put some flowers in pots on the stairs and on the farmer's porch. We can put our rocking chairs here to sit during the day to enjoy our flowers and the peace and quiet. I don't hear anything here though, not even a peep from birds or crickets."

"Yes, I noticed that too. It is almost too still."

"Are you ready to go inside?" the realtor asked.

"Yes, I think we are. The yard is nice and well maintained. Is someone taking care of it?"

"Not that I know of. It has been for sale for many years."

"Oh, I wonder why the grass hasn't grown then?" Calvin stated, puzzled.

"I don't know, sir. I can find out for you though. Maybe someone is taking care of it. It could be part of the conservation area."

"Let's look inside. I will let you know about the land later if you decide to purchase the house."

"Okay," the couple agreed and went inside.

What they saw was shocking. It looked as if someone had been living there. Everything was dust free and polished to a shine. The kitchen appliances were clean and newer than expected. The living room had a comfortable-looking couch with no sagging cushions, and a sturdy lounge chair. The lamps were absent of fringe and were attractive along with the oblong mahogany coffee table.

The couple kept moving throughout the house into the bedroom. The bed was made with a flowered comforter and plenty of pillows graced the headboard, free of any stains.

The bathroom had a clean toilet, sink, and a deep claw foot tub with a shower beside it. Toilet paper hung from the roll that looked fresh and newly replaced. There were even towels hanging from the towel bars that were perfectly aligned and ready for use.

The realtor was behind them taking all this in and finally said, "I can't believe how clean and well-maintained this place is for being so long uninhabited."

"It is strange," Calvin agreed. "But we like it. It is just what we were looking for."

Amelia beamed in agreement and hugged her husband. "Can we buy it, dear?"

"I don't see why not? We need to sell our other place first. Can you help us with that?" He looked to the realtor for her reply.

"I would be happy to do that. Let's go back to my office and we can draw up the papers. I will have to look at your present place and give you an estimate. I have a few people who are looking for a place in the city. It shouldn't be too difficult to sell."

"It is much too big for us now. It has three bedrooms, two that we haven't used since our kids grew up, a large kitchen, dining room, two bathrooms, a spacious living room and a room in the basement that I finished when I was younger. We don't go down there now. It is too problematic to go up and down the stairs. Our two children used the basement until they moved out many years ago. We don't see them too often now."

After the couple and realtor left the house, the squatters who were hiding out in the basement sighed. "I can't believe someone is going to purchase this house," Harry said.

"I know, after all the work we did to make it a home us. Now we are going to lose it," Mara stated, with a sad expression of defeat.

"Don't worry, Mara. We will not lose it for long. We can drive them out. I guess we did too good a job of fixing it up."

"But we never thought anyone would want to buy it all the way out here in the conservation area."

"What do you plan to do, Harry? They will be moving in as soon as they sell their present house."

Harry whispered to Mara and she nodded in agreement. "Sounds good to me. It just may work. After all, they are old and can be easily upset by sounds, evidence of what they said to the realtor. They are going to get anything but peace and quiet here."

***

A month later, the old couple had sold their house and moved into their country home. Things were peaceful as they settled in. They had sold most of their furniture and only brought with them items that they had from when they were first married – a rocking chair and stool, Amelia's sewing machine table and chair, and a China cabinet that was her mother's. They also moved in their fairly new washer and dryer into the roomy bathroom that had the connections already there.

They had stocked the refrigerator, put away their dishes, the pots and pans into the cabinets, towels and sheets in the linen closet, and their clothes and belongings into the closets and bureaus. They washed all the bed linens and comforter that were on the bed. By this time, they were utterly exhausted and needed to retire for the night after a quick dinner of chicken and rice with broccoli. They put the leftovers into the refrigerator, washed up and went to bed.

In the middle of the night, they heard noises coming from the basement. It sounded like someone moving around.

Amelia woke up Calvin and asked him to go see what was causing that noise. He grudgingly got up and put on his slippers and robe and grabbed a flashlight to do the inspection. He wasn't sure that he would be able to go down the stairs but at least he could use the flashlight to look down there from the top of the stairs.

Calvin flipped on the light but it didn't work. Lucky for him he had the flashlight which he focused down the stairs and back and forth as far as he could to see if there was an animal down there. He would have to somehow change the lightbulb or get someone to change it for him.

He could not see anything and all was quiet. He returned to bed and told Amelia that all was well, but she was now sleeping soundly. She didn't hear him but he shrugged and went back to sleep himself.

A short time later the sound was louder. It sounded as if someone was banging the pipes and opening and slamming doors.

Calvin got up once again and looked around. There was no one inside the house, doors were locked, and windows shut tight. He shook his head, sighed and returned to bed.

Every two hours this kept happening. Amelia sat up in bed and said, "Do you want me to go see what is causing all that ratchet?"

"No, dear. I already checked it out three times. There is nothing or no one around. I can't figure out what is making all that noise. I can't believe we came out to the country to sleep away from the noises of the city and here we are up half the night. Maybe it wasn't such a good idea to move here."

"Does that mean you want to move back to the city, Calvin?"

"Well, at least there I knew what was making all the noise. Here, I don't know."

Down in the basement the squatters laughed. It looked like their plan was working.

After many sleepless nights the old couple went to visit the realtor to share their problems about the house.

"I don't understand. There is no one living there but you two. Maybe something in the boiler is making all that noise. You should get it checked out."

The next day they had someone check out the boiler. He also changed the lightbulb so he could see his way downstairs. The maintenance man said that the boiler was in good condition. But he did mention that there was stuff around the basement that looked like someone was living down there.

"What do you mean?" Calvin asked.

"There are a mattress and food down there. I didn't see anyone around though. Have you been downstairs?"

"No, we can't do stairs anymore," Calvin replied.

"Well, maybe you better get someone to clean it all out. It's quite a mess."

Many days went by with the same noises each night. Now the couple noticed that their food was dwindling faster than they could replace it.

"It looks like we have someone stealing our food, Calvin. We know it can't be mice."

"I agree. Maybe I better go downstairs and check this out for myself. I will take my time, one step at a time, Amelia. You don't have to worry."

"I will wait at the top of the stairs for you, Calvin. Please be careful."

Calvin took one step at a time and had almost gotten to the bottom when he slipped and fell the rest of the way down.

Amelia called out, "Calvin, are you all right?"

There was no answer.

She carefully took one step at a time on the stairs as the lights went out. Amelia, as Calvin had done, tripped and fell down the rest of the flight landing next to Calvin.

The squatters watched all this play out and were too frightened to do anything. What they saw next was too difficult to comprehend. As the light went out in the basement, they had hidden behind the boiler when they heard the footsteps of the man as he tripped and fell down the stairs. Next the wife did the same thing. They watched in horror as two images emerged from the shadows and bent down to entwine the hands of the couple and lay them side by side.

"Are you seeing this, Harry?"

"Yes, I can't believe my eyes. Are they ghosts?"

"I...I guess so. I think I want to get out of here now. This is no place to live, Harry."

"Wait until the ghosts disappear and we can run out as fast as we can and never come back. We can find another home to squat in."

Mara nodded and held onto him as they hopped over the bodies, rushed up the stairs, and out the front door.

***

Several days later after the realtor couldn't reach the couple by phone, she went to check on them. When she arrived at the house, all was quiet. She knocked on the door a few times and called out to them. When they didn't answer she used the extra key she had brought to give them.

She kept calling them as she went from room to room with no sign of them. Their bed was unmade, which looked like they did sleep there. She went over to the basement door which was opened and looked down. What she saw was shocking. There at the bottom of the stairs lay the old couple with hands linked together, side by side. She called the police and ambulance, not sure if the couple were alive or dead.

Once the ambulance arrived, they determined that the couple were indeed deceased with no noticeable injuries except each had a head bruise most likely from their falls.

The realtor sighed and said in a whisper, "I should have told them about the other couple who had died like this. This couple was said to haunt the house."

"I don't know about ghosts," the EMT replied when he heard her whisper, "but they do look peaceful."

"I guess so. They said they planned to be together and wished for a place to live out their lives. It looks like they found it," the realtor commented.

"Yes, it does," the EMT responded.

"But maybe the city wasn't such a bad place to be after all," she added.

THE END

A TEEN'S LIFE

A wish can be granted in the strangest of ways.

CHAPTER 1

The teen was unhappy with his life. Every time he tried to do some sport or other activity in school, he failed. He was ready to give up until one day his life changed.

Maybe I better start at the beginning. Marcus was a plain kid who had brown hair and brown eyes but with nothing special about his features or body. He was a little overweight, not obese, but he saw himself as ugly and fat. Each day he buried his head in his computer games to forget about his troubles.

His parents did all they could to encourage him to keep trying to do something new at which they hoped he would finally succeed. They feared for his lack of self-confidence and self-respect. They told him all the time how special he was, to no avail. He didn't believe them, and thought, *what else were they going to say? He was their son. They were supposed to feel like that.*

Marcus had had a particular dreadful day in school. He hadn't felt like going but was forced to attend to take a math test. Math wasn't his best subject but he got by with B's and C's. This time though, he was distracted by a new girl in class who was so striking he couldn't take his eyes off of her. Therefore, he didn't finish the test in time.

He didn't look forward to sharing this poor grade with his parents and see the disappointment mirrored on their faces. He took his time walking home from school which was only half a mile away. He needed the time to come up with the reason why he had failed.

He had ignored all the daily texts he received from students in his class who consistently made fun of him. Instead of dwelling on his grade and the texts he would turn to his video games for comfort. But that was not to be because his parents had other ideas.

When Marcus finally arrived home, his mother and father were there to greet him with wide smiles. He was perplexed by their effusive happiness while he was feeling miserable.

They held a large box in front of them and handed it to him as soon as he came into the kitchen.

"What is this?" Marcus asked, confused and not at all open to surprises in his fickle mood.

"Open it up. Did you forget that tomorrow is your birthday?" his mother queried.

"Oh, right. I did forget." Marcus took the box from his father's hands and was surprised by its weight.

"Aren't you curious about what it is?" his mother asked.

"I guess." Marcus put the box down and sat on the kitchen chair.

"Well, we are waiting. This is an early birthday gift, Marcus. We have some other things for you too," his father continued.

"I see. Thank you." Marcus turned to leave the room.

"Where are you going? Aren't you even a little curious about the gift?" his father stressed.

"Can I open it later? I had a bad day at school and don't feel like looking at it now."

His parents exchanged worried expressions and followed him into his room.

"What's wrong, Marcus? What happened today in school that made you so upset?" his father began.

"I don't want to talk about it, Dad. I am a failure. I should never have been born."

"Now, son, that is not true. You are an intelligent and good-looking young man with great potential."

"Do you really believe that, Dad? You are my father, that is why you are saying that. I know how much I fail all the time at everything. I wish I...."

"What do you wish for?" his mother asked.

"I don't know. I just want to be better looking, smarter, and able to succeed at something. I'd like to have a friend and a girlfriend too," Marcus sighed and laid down on his bed putting his pillow over his head.

His parents sighed heavily and left the box next to his bed.

"Things will get better, Marcus. You wait and see. Okay? Open your present when you feel like it," his father said as he patted his son on his back before leaving the room.

Marcus was drifting off to sleep when he heard a sound coming from the box next to his bed. He leaned over to pull up the cover that was not fixed in any way. He hadn't noticed that before. When the cover was completely lifted, a brown furry head popped out.

He jumped back in surprise but quickly lifted the dog out of the box. It was looking back at him with wide brown eyes and a large tongue that hung down to its chest. This tongue began to lap Marcus all over his face and hands.

Marcus couldn't help but laugh at the dog's tenacity to keep licking his face. He pulled the dog away from his face and hugged it to his chest to calm it down. It was as excited to meet Marcus as he was shocked to see it.

He couldn't believe that his parents had bought him a dog. What was he supposed to do with a dog?

The dog sat down on his lap and turned its head this way and that as if it comprehended what Marcus was thinking.

"What am I supposed to do with you?"

The dog appeared to be smiling at him.

"What? Do you understand me?"

The dog nodded its brown furry head.

"You've got to be kidding me? What are you?"

The dog settled down further on the bed and looked back at Marcus and said, "I am a Labrador retriever, and I am also your confidence. It appears that you need some desperately."

Marcus stared in shock at the dog. "How is this possible? You can talk? Am I hallucinating?" He jumped up from his bed and began walking around the room shaking his head in disbelief.

The dog laid down on the bed now and kept its eyes on Marcus as he paced back and forth.

"What you do depends on you, Marcus. I am here to help you in any way I can. Now where do we start?"

Marcus opened his door and ran out of the room to find his parents. They were sitting at the table having a cup of coffee and discussing something, probably him.

"Mom, Dad, where did you get this dog?"

"Oh, do you like your present?" his mother asked him with a wide smile.

"I...I...can't believe it!"

"Does that mean you like him?" his father queried.

"It just talked to me! Did you know that it can talk?"

His parents exchanged wary expressions with him and waited for Marcus to explain what he just said.

"It is a he, Marcus," his father announced with a grin.

"Okay, but did you know that he can talk?"

"Marcus, are you feeling okay?" his mother asked, with deep concern etched on her face.

"I am not kidding, Mom! He talked to me. He said he was my confidence."

"Did he now?" his father snickered, as he went back to drinking his coffee.

"I don't believe it! You think I have lost my mind, don't you?"

"Not at all, honey. We thought you needed a friend and what better friend than a dog. I used to talk to my dogs too. They were the best listeners," his father responded.

"Oh, never mind. I will deal with this."

Marcus went back to see the dog. Maybe he was just imagining that he talked to him.

The dog was fast asleep on the bed when Marcus came into his room. He laid down next to the dog and found that he was tired enough to sleep too.

When Marcus woke an hour later, he found the dog cuddled up to him and snoring loudly. That is probably what woke him up.

He petted the dog who sighed and stirred. The dog opened his eyes and looked at Marcus as he began to lick Marcus' face once again.

"Okay, that is enough. I don't need another bath. Now tell me, did you really talk to me before?" He waited for the dog to respond but he was quiet.

"I guess I am going crazy. You can't talk. I must have imagined what you did before."

"No, you didn't imagine anything, Marcus. I can talk. Now tell me about yourself and what concerns you."

"I…I…don't know what to say? I've never spoken to a dog before!"

"Well, there is always a first time. You will be the only one who can hear me speak. If you try to ask me to talk to anyone else all they will hear is a bark or two."

"Why is that? How come I can hear you?"

"I heard that you had a wish and I was sent here to help you. Now what is your wish?"

"Who sent you?"

"Someone who loves you."

"Who is that?"

"HE loves everyone. Now stop messing around and explain yourself. What do you want?"

"If I tell you, will you be able to grant my wishes?"

"Wishes? Who said anything about wishes?" the dog smirked at him.

"Well, I have more than one wish, that is why. I have so many issues that I can't think straight."

"Hmm. I see but I can't help you there. You must come up with just one wish. That is all I can grant from HIM."

"There you go again with HIM! I don't get it? Who is HE? No one loves me, well, maybe my parents do. But that is because they are supposed to love me, right?"

"I wouldn't know anything about that. I don't have parents. I guess I did at one time but I don't remember them."

"That must mean you are an orphan."

"Maybe I am. But now I have you as a friend and you have me."

"I suppose you are right there. Can you do any tricks, dog?"

"No, I do not do any tricks. What do you think I am, a monkey?"

"Sorry, I didn't want to insult you. What's wrong with monkeys anyway?"

"Nothing really, but they do tricks for peanuts. That is way below me. Oh, by the way, I am hungry and thirsty."

"Oh, I forgot. What would you like to eat?"

"Do you have any hamburgers or hot dogs? I especially love hot dogs raw, not cooked."

"Okay, let's go get one for you. Do you have to go outside to do…you know…?"

"Yes, I will after I eat and drink. That is kind of you to ask, Marcus."

The dog followed Marcus out of his room to the kitchen where his parents were still sitting. They looked up with smiles at Marcus who appeared to be feeling better and happy with his gift.

"What are you going to name your dog, Marcus?" his father asked.

"I don't know yet. I will have to ask him what name he would like."

His parents chuckled at his comment and kept their eyes on Marcus and the dog as they went to the refrigerator.

"What are you giving him, Marcus?" his mother asked.

"He said he likes hot dogs."

"Really? He told you that?" his mother giggled.

"Is that okay if I give him a couple?"

"Sure, whatever makes him happy, Marcus," his mother stated with a nod.

"Don't forget to take him out to relieve himself and for a walk. He needs exercise," his father added.

"I plan to do that after he eats."

The dog gobbled up two hot dogs and drank a bowl full of water before barking to be let outside.

"See, he told you that he needs to go out," his mother said.

What Marcus heard from the dog was, 'Take me outside now.'

Marcus walked his dog around the neighborhood which caused others to stop, pet it, and ask what was its name.

"I just got him but I haven't named him yet. Still thinking about that."

The dog looked up at Marcus and responded, "I kind of like Tiger myself."

"Tiger? You are anything but a tiger!" Marcus responded with a titter.

"Why? Just because I don't have stripes? Is that it? Okay, well, how about Lion? I do have brown hair like a lion."

Marcus laughed out loud and said, "No, not lion either. I've been thinking."

"I don't like the sound of that, Marcus! Please don't say Rover or Mike! Those names are so lame!"

"I got the perfect name for you - Zeus!"

"Zeus? What kind of name is that?"

"Well, Zeus was an Olympic God. He was a powerful and tyrannical ruler. The name also evokes strength, wisdom and grace."

"Hmm, let me think this over. I need to say it a few times in my head to get used to it. Now you need to call me by that name to see if I respond."

"Hey, Zeus! Come here, Zeus!"

The dog did not move and then turned away.

"Where are you going, Zeus?"

"I'm not used to it yet. Try it again."

"Zeus, here Zeus!"

"Oh, all right. I accept the name. Now let's go home. I want a snack after all this walking. Besides, we have a lot to discuss, Marcus. Now head home."

"Hey, you are not the boss here, Zeus. You have to listen to me! Let's go home."

Zeus wore a broad grin and strutted home.

When they got back home, Marcus opened up his computer to play his games.

"What are you doing, Marcus?"

"Oh, just playing some games."

"What kind of games?" Zeus asked trying to look over Marcus' shoulder.

"Nothing that would interest you, Zeus."

"Really, how do you know?"

"Can you read?"

"Well, not really, but I could figure it out. Why don't you take me outside and play ball with me instead? That is something I am quite good at."

"All right, just for a little while."

A little while turned out to be a couple of hours. By the time they came inside it was dinner time and Marcus had to finish up his homework. He found that he hadn't missed his computer games at all.

CHAPTER 2

Marcus looked forward to returning home each day to discuss what had transpired at school with Zeus. Zeus always had something positive to add and some keen insight into many things.

Marcus had passed all his math tests since the last one and even did some extra work to compensate for his failing grade after discussing this with his teacher.

The new girl was paying more attention to him and even asked if he would walk her home one day. Marcus looked forward to having company on his walk home.

Zeus was waiting at the front steps when Marcus came home looking pleased with himself.

"What are you smiling about, Marcus? Did you get to have some hot dogs?"

"No, silly, Zeus. I like hot dogs but not as much as you do. I just walked Sondra home from school. She is the new girl in my homeroom class I told you about."

"Oh, I see. She likes you?"

"Maybe a little. She is something else!"

"What else?"

"That is just a saying, Zeus. It means she is special."

"Oh, okay. I can understand that. I saw a cute dog on our walk recently that I would like to get to know."

"What?"

"I guess that you are not interested in what I like."

"Hmm? What did you say, Zeus?"

"Never mind. I guess our little talks have worked wonders on you, Marcus. I see you have grown in confidence."

"Have I? I haven't noticed."

"Well, you are not moping around and complaining anymore, your grades are improving and you are also not playing those stupid computer games anymore. That is a good thing, right?"

"Yes, my parents are happy with my last report card. But I still have not received my wish."

"Wish? What wish?"

"When you first spoke to me you promised me one wish."

"I did?"

Marcus shook his head and sighed. "I can't believe that I am talking to you. You must have a short memory or just want to drive me crazy."

"No, I don't have to do that. You were doing that to yourself before I came. Now you seem a little more… normal."

"What do you know about normal in human terms?"

"I really don't but that is what I perceive."

"You perceive? Do you even know what that means, Zeus?"

"I'm not sure, but I think I am right."

"Maybe you are or maybe you aren't."

"What's new with you, Marcus? Do you have any concerns that you want to discuss with me?"

"No. Well, maybe one."

"What's that?"

"I need to ask Sondra to the senior dance but don't know how to do that."

"Well, just ask her."

"What am I doing asking a dog about how to go on a date with a girl? What do you know about such things?"

"I don't know anything about that but I do know how to ask a dog if she would like to…."

"Stop right there! I don't want to hear about such things!"

"What things? I was only going to say that I would ask a female of my kind to go for a walk or pee at a certain place together."

"Do you really do that?"

"Sure, why not? We mark our territory together so no other male will go near my girl."

"Oh my god, I don't believe I am listening to you!"

"Don't you do such things? Go to the bathroom in the same room?"-

"Well, yes, but not at the same time," Marcus sighed.

"Whatever."

CHAPTER 3

Marcus decided to ask Sondra to the dance the next day after much thought. He only hoped that she would say yes. She seemed to be enjoying his company on their walks home each day. That was a start.

When he arrived at school, he noticed a large sign had gone up about the dance and another smaller one about field and track tryouts. There was a sign-up sheet on the bulletin board as he went inside where several boys and girls were signing up.

He stood back and waited for everyone to clear away so he could get closer and maybe sign up himself. He held a pen in his hand and stared at the sheet with many names already listed.

A boy was behind him and tapped him on the shoulder. "Are you going to sign up or not?"

"I…I…guess so. Sorry for holding you up."

"That's all right. I feel the same way. I don't know if I will make it or not but at least I will try. My name is Carlson. What's yours?"

"I'm Marcus. I think I have seen you around, Carlson. Nice to meet you."

"Same here. Have you tried out before, Marcus?"

"Yeah, I've tried out for a lot of sports but never made a team. Maybe this time I will make it."

"That is the way to feel. I keep trying too. One day I will make it also. Maybe we will be on the same team. That would be great, right?"

"Most definitely it would be."

"See you around, Marcus."

"Yeah, you too, Carlson."

When Marcus got to homeroom, Sondra was sitting there looking like an angel with her golden hair shining in the light. He gulped back a sigh and sat down and looked her way. She smiled back at him and turned her attention to the teacher as class began.

Marcus waited all day for a chance to talk to her alone. He finally saw her in the hall outside her locker and rushed over to talk to her. This was his chance.

As he was closing in on her, Carlson appeared at his side. "Hi, Marcus. How are you doing? Did you pass that science quiz today?"

"Umm, hi Carlson. I need to see someone. Can I talk to you later?"

"Ah, sure. Whatever." Carlson hung his head and moped away.

Marcus felt bad about doing that but he had to ask Sondra now before someone else did.

Sondra looked up at him as he stood beside her. "Hi Marcus. What's happening?"

"Hi Sondra. I...I...was wondering if you would like to...to go to the dance next weekend."

"Sure! I would love to go with you, Marcus. What time are you going to pick me up?"

Marcus couldn't believe his ears. She had said yes!

"Marcus, did you hear me?"

"Yes, you said yes. I heard you. Great! I will pick you up at 6:00. Okay?"

"Okay, see you then. I mean, I will see you after school on our walk home." Sondra smiled and waved to him as she walked to her next class.

"Wow! I did it! Wait till I tell Zeus about that! He won't believe it!"

Marcus quickly met up with Carlson to apologize for dismissing him and planned a time for them to get together after school one day. Carlson was happy to agree and the two went to their next class with their heads held high.

After walking from school, Marcus dropped off Sondra at her house and headed home, he didn't see Zeus waiting for him on the front porch. Where was he? He called his name as he entered the house but only saw his mother in the kitchen and no sign of Zeus.

"Hi Mom. Where is Zeus?"

"I don't know dear. He was outside a little while ago."

"Okay. I'll go look for him."

Marcus looked all afternoon and well into the night with no sign of him anywhere. He was getting worried and feeling lost and alone once again without his best friend.

He finally came in and ate dinner after his mother's urging and went to his room to do his homework.

What he found in his room was Zeus' toys and blanket where he slept and a note on his desk. It said, "Had to leave you now that you are well, whole again, and normal. I need to help another boy now. Nice to know you, Marcus. Remember to always believe in yourself and that you can do anything when you stay positive."

Marcus dropped the note back onto his desk and held his head in his hands as his eyes filled with unspent tears. He couldn't believe Zeus had left him or that he had written this letter!

He never did grant me a wish, or did he?

THE END

THE MAGICAL PEBBLE

Sometimes hardship can spring with unexpected blessings.

The teenager had walked a mile in her shoes with holes. Her feet were aching but she had to get to work on time or she would lose her job.

Her stepfather had told her that she better bring home enough tips to cover some of the bills that were piling up with her mother being sick.

Shiloh couldn't believe the nerve of her stepfather to say that to her. He didn't work and couldn't hold onto a job because of all his drinking. No wonder her mother got sick from his behavior and the beatings she took to protect her children.

There were three other children in the family. Shiloh was the oldest at sixteen. Her twin brothers were ten and her sister was eight.

Shiloh worried about them and always helped her mother care for them when her mother couldn't. She had no life of her own since her father died and her mother married this bum. She even had to drop out of school to get a job. She only wished her life was different.

She suddenly stumbled over a rock that got stuck in the hole in her shoe. She tried to ignore it but it only dug into her heel even more. She stopped to take it out but couldn't budge it.

"That's strange. Why won't it come out?"

Before she could move any further, a light appeared in front of her and a beautiful lady all in blue stepped out and looked at her. The lady smiled at Shiloh and pointed to her shoe. "Don't worry about the pebble. Soon things will get better for you and your family."

Shiloh blinked and wiped her eyes. When she opened them again, the lady had disappeared. She must be hallucinating. *Did I really see a lady?*

She hobbled the rest of the way to work and would try to work out the pebble later when she had a break. Her boss would not understand why she was late if she told him she had to stop and remove a pebble from her shoe. Forget about seeing a lady. It all sounded lame and unbelievable even to her.

Shiloh worked all day and finally when her break came, she grabbed a quick meal and removed her shoe. The pebble was not there but her shoe no longer had holes in it either. In fact, it looked brand new and so did the other one.

How did this happen? She did notice that her feet had not been hurting her in spite of all the walking back and forth around the restaurant and to and from the kitchen. She had forgotten how much pain she had been in previously. But now this was strange in a good way. Someone must be looking out for her.

She felt her spirits improve and walked with a lighter and carefree step. She felt upbeat even when her boss called her about an order that had been slow to be delivered to a customer.

She smiled and nodded as she brought over the order and apologized to the man who gave her a bigger tip than she expected. In fact, her tips were larger than usual all around.

When she arrived home, she found her mother up and about preparing dinner and no sign of her stepfather. He was probably out drinking somewhere.

"How are you feeling, Mom?"

"I'm doing much better, Shiloh. How was work?"

"Better than usual. Something strange happened to me that I would like to share with you. Also, my tips are great. I'll put them away so that he won't find them."

"Good idea, sweetheart. What was so strange today?"

Shiloh helped her mother prepare dinner as she explained about the pebble in her shoe, the lady who appeared in front of her and what she had said.

"Let me see those shoes."

Shiloh took off her shoes and showed her mother the sole which looked like it was brand new.

"Wow! They do look new, Shiloh. How can that be?"

"I don't know, Mom, but it's a good thing, right. Maybe someone is watching over me."

"The lady was probably your Guardian Angel. We all have one or are supposed to, that is."

"It looks like yours is watching over you too, Mom. You look healthy today. You even have some color in your cheeks."

"Do I? That is good. I had been feeling miserable lately until today shortly after you left for work."

"Really? That is strange. The pebble that got into my shoe happened not long after I was walking. I had to walk the rest of the way to work with it pinching my foot but there wasn't any blood."

"Let's just be happy that something good came to us today. We can only hope that it keeps coming our way. Now get your brothers and sister to wash up for dinner. It's almost ready."

"Sure thing, Mom." Shiloh ran around looking for the kids and found them in the backyard digging holes.

"What are you doing? Mom won't be happy with all these holes."

"We found a pretty stone and the more we dig we keep finding more. Look at them!"

Shiloh bent down to look at all the colorful stones that her siblings had uncovered. "They are beautiful! Let's bring them inside and wash them off. You can keep them on your bookshelves. Mom wants you to come in now and get cleaned up for dinner."

The three children grabbed all the stones and hurried inside to wash them and themselves. They were excited to share them with their mother.

The twins were born with cerebral palsy but managed to get around slowly with limps and shaky hands. The youngest sibling did all she could at her young age to help them along even though her eyesight was not perfect.

When all the children were sitting at the table, their mother noticed that the boys were sitting up straighter and smiling. Their faces were not fixed as usual in a frown.

"How are you feeling, boys?"

The twins perked up and said clear as day, "We are feeling really good today, Mom!"

They always answered together and never did anything alone. They were inseparable. That's how twins are.

Their mother smiled and patted them on their heads as she looked up to the ceiling and said, "Thanks."

Shiloh nodded to her too and winked. "I guess we all have Guardian Angels today."

The youngest daughter looked at her hands and noticed that they were still a little dirty. "Look, Mom! I missed a spot of dirt."

"What did you say, sweetheart?" her mother asked.

"I missed a spot on my hand."

"Let me see," her mother looked at her daughter's hand and saw a tiny spot of dirt. She grabbed her daughter and hugged her fiercely.

"What's wrong, Mom?"

"You can see this tiny spot, sweetie?"

"Yes, Mom. I can see clearly. I never could before."

"That's right. You never could. Well, that is another thing to be thankful for," her mother said, in surprise and relied.

After dinner there was still no sign of the children's stepfather. They had gone to bed and locked their door, per their mother's orders, for fear that he would disturb them in some way. He was not to be trusted when he was drunk.

The next morning there was still no sign of her husband when she woke to make breakfast.

"Shiloh, can you please get the children up now and ready for breakfast?"

"Sure, Mom. Where is my stepfather?"

"I don't know. He never came home last night."

"Oh?"

"He is probably sleeping off the booze somewhere. Don't worry about him. He will find his way back here. He always does."

"I guess so. Maybe we will have a better day today without him, Mom."

"Maybe," her mother said with a deep sigh.

The children came out of their rooms before Shiloh could get them. The boys were walking tall and straight and their hands were still. Their little sister was reading a book and laughing.

Shiloh stood there in awe watching them healthy and strong and seeing well. She couldn't believe her eyes.

Each child held onto a colorful stone that they had found outside the day before.

Shiloh tried to take the stones from their hands but they did not let go. "You can put the stones down on the table while you eat."

"No, we were told if we always kept them close to us, we would be well."

"Who told you that?" their mother asked.

"The lady."

"What lady?"

"The lady in the stones."

"What?" their mother asked in disbelief.

"What did the lady look like?" Shiloh asked her sister.

"She was beautiful and was dressed all in blue."

Shiloh nodded and exchanged wide-eyed expressions with her mother.

Their mother took the stone from her daughter's hand to examine it closely. When she did this, her daughter cried out, "I can't see, Mom!"

"What do you mean you can't see?"

"I can't see clearly like I do if I have the stone in my hand."

Shiloh took the stones and put them into her brothers' pockets and one in her sister's pocket. At once they felt better.

"You need to keep them in your pockets, that's all. You don't need to hold onto them. I think that is what the lady meant."

The three children nodded and ate their breakfast checking their pockets every few minutes.

Many days went by without any sign of their stepfather. Shiloh was doing well at work and had been given a raise for her exceptional work and attitude. Everyone raved about her and how sweet she was when she greeted them and brought their orders.

Her mother was healthy and now looking for a job to help out while the children were in school.

Shiloh was taking a class after work to get her GED. Now she could get her diploma, find a better job, and possibly work her way through college one day.

She thought over the day that she had stepped on that pebble and her siblings had found the colorful stones. Their lives had changed for the better. *Isn't that what the lady said? Our lives would get better. Maybe she really was our guardian angel.*

THE END

ONE MORE CHANCE

Sometimes things happen in life that can't be explained but they give you the chance to begin again.

The homeless Vet pulled the newspaper over his body to keep out the chill. He would have to find something warmer than paper to survive the cold weather that would soon be moving in. He had on his Army cap and fatigues. That was all the clothes he owned now.

He lay there and fell asleep, finding himself back in Afghanistan. Gunfire was getting closer to him and his buddies. One of them was his best friend, Fraser. He called out to them to get down but they couldn't hear him with all the noise from the guns and explosions around them.

He shuddered when in the next second a bomb landed next to his buddies and blew them away. He had crawled away just in time into another hole that had protected him. But he found himself covered in their blood.

He woke in a sweat even in the cold as he shuddered to erase the dream from his mind. He couldn't sleep each day because this dream kept coming back to him. If only he could have warned his buddies sooner.

When he got out of the service, he had tried to find a job but he jeopardized each job he had by his PTSD. He couldn't concentrate because he was so tired all the time and eventually lost each job he had.

He had lived on the street until someone kicked him off and he had to move once again. He was now under a bridge with countless others who were also lost.

He sat up and looked around. He would have to find something to eat soon. He hadn't eaten in two days and was trying to survive on water and an occasionally tossed half-eaten sandwich that he grabbed out of the trash can.

What kind of life is this? He had to look for another job. All he needed was one more chance. Would someone out there be willing to give it to him?

A well-dressed man walked by and met his eye. He came over to the Vet and stopped in front of him. Are you hungry?"

The Vet looked shocked to see someone actually speaking to him. He looked dirty, bedraggled and probably gave off a horrific body odor that could fell an elephant.

"Me? Are you talking to me?"

"Yes, I am. You were in the service?"

"Yes, I was in the Army and served in Afghanistan."

"Hmm. I see. My brother did that too. He didn't make it home though. You were one of the lucky ones, I guess."

"Well, maybe, but look at me now!"

"Come with me. I'll buy you lunch or dinner or whatever you want. I would like to hear more about your time in the Army."

"I don't understand. I appreciate the meal, mister, but why do you want to know more about my service?"

"Just curious, I guess. I never got to talk to my brother."

"Oh, I'm sorry about your brother."

"We're going to make one stop before we go to eat. You need to freshen up a little."

"I am pretty ripe, right? Sorry about that. I have no place to shower or any clothes to change into even if I did shower somewhere."

The man led the Vet to an apartment a short distance away. It was on the seventh floor in a swanky building.

The Vet's eyes widened when they entered the luxurious apartment. It had highly polished wood floors, expensive furniture, and paintings on the walls that look as if they came out of a museum. He couldn't stop gawking at everything around him. Also, it was meticulously clean unlike him. He didn't dare touch anything.

"I think my brother's clothes will fit you. I'm sorry I don't even know your name. I'm Ethan. What's yours?"

"Gregory, but everyone calls me Greg. Is this your place?"

"Yes. It was also where my brother lived. I didn't throw away any of his clothes or things and his room is as it was before he left for the Army. I couldn't do that yet. It was long ago, but I am still having a difficult time with his loss. He was a special kind of guy. He was kind, caring and always thought of everyone but himself. I am nothing like him."

"I wouldn't say that. Look, you picked up a bum like me to feed and clothe. You can't be too bad, Ethan."

"I…I…am working on changing since his death. I have everything I could ever want but really feel lost. Money or things can't make you happy."

"I would like a little money to find that out," Greg responded.

"Let's get you cleaned up and dressed so we can go out to eat. Okay? The bathroom is this way. I will get you some clothes to change into after you shower. Towels, shampoo and everything is in there. Let me know if you need anything else."

Greg nodded and went into the bathroom and came back a short time later fresh, clean and renewed. He found Ethan sitting on the couch with his head in his hands.

"Are you all right, Ethan?"

"Oh, you are done already? That was quick. Yeah, I'm fine. Just reliving the day that I received the letter from the service from my brother. It was the last time I heard from him. The next time it was two men in uniforms at my door to tell me that he was gone."

"Oh, I can't imagine how hard that must have been for you. Do you have any other family?"

"No, it was only my brother and me. We lost our parents tragically several years ago in a car accident by a drunk driver. I don't think they could have survived this news of my brother's death. It would have been the death of them."

Greg didn't know what else to say. He waited a moment and cleared his throat.

"Oh, I'm sorry again. Let's go eat. You must be hungry. When was the last time you had a decent meal?"

"Oh, probably a couple of days ago I had a half-eaten sandwich I found." Greg neglected to say where he had found it.

"Well, then we better get going. I know of a great place to go. Do you like Italian food? This was my brother's favorite place to eat when he was home."

"You bet! I like all kinds of food!" Greg's mouth was already watering at the thought of Italian food. He loved meatballs, chicken parm, pasta and of course pizza! He couldn't wait to dig in.

"I don't know how to repay you for your hospitality and kindness, Ethan. I don't have any money and can't keep a job for long."

"Why can't you keep a job, Greg?" Ethan asked as they left the apartment and headed to the garage to pick up his car.

"I have PTSD and nightmares that keep me awake all night. If I can't sleep, I can't function. I have been known to fall asleep on the job."

"That's not a good thing. But if you could manage to sleep through the night you could keep a job."

"Yeah, maybe I could. But how do I get rid of the nightmares?"

"What are the nightmares about – the service?"

"Yeah. Terrible things happen over there that I can't get out of my head."

"I see. I'm sorry, Greg. Here's my car. Hop in. We'll be there in fifteen minutes."

"Thanks, Ethan. Nice car you have here."

"It's a Rolls Royce. I have a computer business that has been quite successful. I would give it all back if I could have my brother back though."

Greg was once again speechless. He didn't know what to say. He sighed and sat there quietly for the rest of the ride.

"We are here, Greg. This isn't a fancy place but I come here often because it reminds me of my brother."

As soon as they entered, the waiter and greeter came to see Ethan and shake his hand. They seated them at a window with a lovely view of the back near a small pond. It was quiet and peaceful. Greg felt at once like he was home and a calm feeling came over him. He watched the ducks swim around on the pond and sighed.

"Do you like this place, Greg?"

"Ahh, yes. It is beautiful and so serene. I feel at peace here."

"That's good to hear. My brother said something very similar to that too when he sat here."

Greg nodded as he looked over the menu trying to keep his gnawing stomach in check. He finally settled on the chicken parm and homemade pasta with a side of meatballs and a salad.

Ethan ordered the same thing and smiled for the first time and said, "That was my brother's favorite meal too. He had quite an appetite. He always finished the whole thing but I brought half of mine home which he would eat later that night or the next day." He chuckled as he watched Greg pick up a slice of crusty bread and lather it with butter, eating most of it in one bite.

"You better take your time and give your stomach a chance to catch up with your mouth, Greg. I don't want to see you sick."

"Of course. I will try to slow down. It is so delicious! I love bread and butter. In fact, I love all kinds of foods."

"That's good. I like to see a man enjoying his food. I never was much for eating big meals but I find myself hungry for the first time."

"Good, because I don't want to be the only one making a pig of myself as I gobble everything in sight," Greg laughed as he stuffed the rest of the bread into his mouth.

"Tell me a little about yourself, Greg. How did you decide that you wanted to go into the Army?"

"I had this best friend in school and he told me about the Army and how I could get my schooling paid for and even get a decent pension for the rest of my life."

"So, did that work out for you? Did you get to finish school? Get your pension?"

"Well, I need to get my pension but don't have an address for them to send it. Also, I don't have the desire to go to college. I can't concentrate long enough to learn anything."

"I can help you get your pension, Greg. Now about college. Maybe that would be a good thing for you to do. At least you would be able to get a job, a good job to get you off the streets."

"I guess so. But where do I start?"

"Let me take care of that. I have many connections that will get you where you need to go. In the meantime, you can work for me in my business."

"Computers? I don't know anything about computers, Ethan. I barely do anything with technology. I don't even have a phone."

"You can always learn."

"My best friend, Fraser, told me that we would go into some kind of business together once we got out of the Army. But unfortunately, he didn't make it."

"Fraser? Your best friend was named Fraser? That is an unusual name."

"Yes, he said his mother's father's name was Fraser. He didn't like it and we had to call him Fray instead."

"Fray? Are you serious, Greg?"

"Yes, why?" Greg looked at the strange expression on Ethan's face and the tears that brimmed in his eyes.

"What is wrong, Ethan? Did I say something wrong?"

"No, not at all, Greg. Fraser was my brother's name and everyone called him Fray."

THE END

THE ROAD TO NOWHERE

This is what they had always wished for – an adventure before beginning a life together. They promised to be together always no matter what happened. They never expected this though.

The couple were traveling to find a new home but their car broke down on a lonely road with nothing in sight. They decided to begin walking until someone came along or they found civilization.

They had gotten married a few days ago and wanted to take a trip somewhere different to begin their new life together as man and wife. This break down of their car was unexpected. The car was not that old and was in good shape. They had checked it over and replaced the oil, filled the tires with air, and cleaned it inside and out.

As they continued to walk, the road seemed to grow in front of them. It was almost as if they weren't moving at all. The man looked behind him and saw their car closer than it should have been after walking for half an hour.

He stopped and looked around. There were no houses or businesses in sight, just woods on both sides of the narrow street.

"What's wrong, Roman?"

"Look behind us, Meara. Our car is closer than it was before we began walking."

"How can that be? We have been moving forward, not backward."

"It doesn't appear that way though, does it?"

"No, not at all. Let's go back to the car and stay inside. At least we can rest until someone comes by to help us."

"What if no one comes by? Are we to just sit here and do nothing but waste away?"

"I don't know, Roman. I am getting tired and will be even more tired if we find ourselves in the same place an hour or more from now."

"Okay, let's go back and rest. Then we can try walking again in a little while."

The couple walked and walked but didn't get any closer to the car. What was going on?

"I don't believe this, Roman. What are we going to do?"

"I have to think this over. Maybe we are dreaming and this is just a nightmare from which we will eventually wake."

"I sure hope so. I don't like not moving like this. It is depressing to say the least. This is supposed to be the start of our life together. In fact, this is our honeymoon. Right?"

"Yes, dear, it is. Don't worry. Let's stop here and sit on the side of the road away from traffic, if and when there is any coming this way, that is. We need to think this over."

The couple sat down next to a large tree and leaned back to rest. Before long they both fell asleep.

The road beneath them moved on its own causing them to wake up. They jumped up and looked for their car. It was no longer there. They were farther up the road than before. Maybe they had walked longer than they thought.

"Where are we now, Roman? I don't see the car. I thought it was close by."

"Yes, so did I. Did you fall asleep too?"

"I think I did. I dreamed that we were moving. It was a strange feeling."

"I felt that too, Meara. That is what woke me up. The road was moving and taking us with it."

"Maybe we better keep walking. The road seems to want us to keep moving."

"Odd as that sounds, Meara, I think you are right. I still think we are in a dream sequence that we can't get out of until something happens to wake us."

"What has to happen? I don't like the sound of that, Roman. Will one of us get injured or maybe die?"

"No, I didn't mean that. I meant that we will eventually come out of our dream and realize that we were dreaming."

"That doesn't even make sense, Roman."

"Nothing else makes sense here either, Meara."

"Okay. What should we do now?"

"I don't have the foggiest," Roman sighed but trudged along at a slow pace.

Look, there is someone ahead! Let's move faster and see if he can help us."

"Is it a he or a she?" Roman asked, wary of any more problems.

"It looks like a man to me, Roman."

"Come on. We can't just stand here. Keep moving. We will meet him sooner or later. He is moving toward us too."

The figure appeared to grow larger as it came closer to them. They stopped and waited for the man to come to them.

The man stopped when they stopped and looked at them but did not speak.

Roman called out to him, "Can you help us?"

The man didn't say anything but turned away.

Meara called out to him, "Wait a minute. Don't go. We are lost and need help."

The man stopped and turned toward them and resumed walking their way.

"What is wrong?" the man responded.

"We need help with our car. It broke down."

The man stopped a few feet in front of them. "Where are you from? How did you come this way?"

The couple looked at each other. "We don't know how we got here. We haven't been able to move too far. We appear to be stuck in one spot. We also don't know where our car is. It has disappeared."

"Hmm, I see. You really don't know where you are?"

"No, we don't. Can you tell us?"

"You need to wait here. HE will be coming to see you."

"Who will be coming to see us?" Roman asked in confusion.

"What is he talking about? Why can't he help us?" Meara queried to no one, for the man had disappeared.

The couple waited and found themselves sleeping once again against the large tree. When they woke, they saw people all around them.

"Who are all these people, Roman?" Meara asked in alarm.

"I don't know. They are just standing here staring at us. "Ask them for help."

"You ask them, Roman. You always promised to take care of me."

"Okay. Hi there, can you assist us in getting our car fixed so we can be on our way?"

They shook their heads and looked behind them.

The couple followed their eyes and saw their car. It was all crunched up as if it had been in an accident.

"Our car, Roman! Look at our car! Someone crashed it! How are we going to go anywhere?"

Roman eyes grew wide as he looked at the car that they had driven a short time ago that had been in good shape. What happened to it?

"I don't know how that could have happened. It was fine a while ago."

They turned back to find that all the people were gone. Now where did they go?

"I don't know what is happening here, Roman. I am frightened."

"I know, Meara. I feel uncomfortable about this too. But there has to be an explanation. Someone has to know something."

A large man was coming their way. HE grew larger and larger until HE towered over them. HE was not menacing but rather exuded a kind aura and had eyes full of empathy as HE looked at them.

The couple were speechless and looked back at the man who wasn't just a man. HE was something more powerful and not from this world.

They waited for the man to speak. They found themselves calmer and no longer frightened or upset.

The man did not speak with HIS mouth but words appeared in their heads as they listened to HIM.

"You are in the wrong place at the wrong time. You were not meant to be here yet. I heard your wish for you to be together always but it is not your time to leave Earth. You must go back now. I will guide you to your place. Close your eyes and you will wake up in your car and continue on your journey. You will have a long life together and never be separated."

"I don't understand. Who are you?" Roman asked in a whisper, afraid to speak loudly in this man's presence.

"You are to go now. There will be a time when you will return together."

"What? Are we dead?" Meara asked, confused.

"No, not yet. Leave now and enjoy your life together."

Roman nodded and told Meara, "Listen to HIM. I know who HE is."

"Okay. But I still don't understand how we got here."

"It doesn't matter now. We will not return to this place for many years. You heard HIM say that."

"Do you mean to say that HE is who I think HE is?"

"Yes, now close your eyes and we will be gone from here."

"Thank God," Meara sighed.

"You're welcome!"

THE END

ONE MISTAKE

Sometimes we make one mistake in life that can change everything. Maybe that mistake can heal and make you and others whole again.

CHAPTER 1

She cried into her pillow after realizing the mistake she had made. What was she going to do?

She had called to tell him that she was pregnant. He didn't respond but hung up instead.

She thought that he loved her, that is why she gave herself to him. What was she thinking? Her parents were going to kill her and most likely kick her out of the house.

She sat up quickly when her bedroom door opened. Her mother stood there and looked at her. "What's wrong, Hope?

Why are you crying? Did your boyfriend break up with you?"

"No, well, maybe he did, Mom."

"Oh, sweetheart. You are so young and have your whole life ahead of you."

"Oh, Mom. I don't know what to do?" Hope cried harder and covered her face with her pillow to soak up the tears that kept coming.

"You need to wipe those tears now and get up. You can help me make a cake for your little sister. Today is Esme's birthday."

"Oh, I forgot! I'm sorry. Of course, I will help you." Hope dried her tears and would deal with this later. Her sister's birthday was more important right now. She would find a way to tell her parents and suffer the consequences for her mistake.

Hope and her mother spent the rest of the afternoon preparing for the birthday party that Esme was going to have. Esme was to stay at her best friend's house until her mother called and told her to come home. Esme knew that her mother was preparing her surprise party, only it wasn't a surprise. She had eavesdropped on her parent's conversation the night before. Esme was excited but kept this to herself. She didn't want to disappoint her parents and would act surprised.

Esme got the message that it was time for her to return home. Her best friend's mother was driving her home which was less than a mile away. She buckled up her seat belt or at least tried to. It wouldn't go into the hole. She didn't tell her friend's mother that she didn't have her seatbelt on. It was only a short distance away anyway.

Esme couldn't stop bouncing around in her seat thinking about her birthday party as they came closer to her house. She wondered what her parents were going to give her as a present. She had asked for a new bike, a ten speed one, like all the bigger girls had. She would grow into it and learn how to use it.

They came to a stop sign and her friend's mother begin to go move through the stop when another car driving too fast came from the other direction and slammed into their car on the side where Esme was seated.

There was a screech of tires as the person who hit them had tried to stop but couldn't because they were under intoxication.

Esme flew up into the air hitting her head first on the roof and again on the door that was now pushed into her.

Her friend's mother was not seriously injured but suffered a neck sprain. When she turned to ask Esme if she was all right, she saw the child's bloodied and broken body lying on the floor of the back seat.

She screamed and tried to open the back door to get to Esme to see if she was alive. Other people around who witnessed the accident called the police and an ambulance right away.

When the ambulance arrived, they removed Esme's body and found a slight pulse. They put her into the ambulance and flew to the nearest hospital in hopes of saving her life.

Esme's friend's mother was checked out by the EMTs who told her to see her doctor and get a thorough checkup after she claimed she was feeling fine. She was more concerned about Esme and couldn't figure out why the child had been out of her seatbelt. She thought Esme had put it on. What was she going to tell the child's mother?

She called Esme's mother and relayed what happened apologizing for not knowing that she did not have her seatbelt on. She said that her husband was going to pick her up and she would go to the hospital, too, to see how Esme was doing.

Esme's mother was hysterical as she listened to her friend explain what happened to her daughter. She called out to her husband and told him about the accident and that Esme was critical.

Hope and her parents drove to the hospital to see their daughter and sister and prayed all the way there that she would survive. This was anything but a happy day for their young daughter who was now eight years old.

When they arrived, the parents rushed to the emergency room desk to inquire about their daughter. The nurse looked up from her phone call and raised her hand to signal one minute.

They paced back and forth in front of the nurses' station with grief written all over their faces. The nurse finally put down the phone and the parents both spoke at once. She raised her hand again and pointed to one of them to answer.

Esme's mother answered and pleaded, "Please let us see our daughter, Esme. She was just admitted to the hospital after a car accident. Today is her birthday. She is only eight years old."

The nurse quickly directed the family back to one of the cubicles where Esme was being treated. She said, "You can see her but please do not get in the way of the staff so that they can treat her."

They nodded numbly and looked in on their daughter and sister who was lying there covered in blood on her face and hooked up to IVs. The doctor tended to her and requested x-rays and other tests after his examination.

"Are you the parents of Esme?"

"Yes, we are. Is she going to be all right, doctor?" her father asked with a heavy heart.

"We don't know the extent of her internal injuries yet. She is breathing on her own but may have some broken ribs, collar bone and a concussion. We will be doing some x-rays and keeping a close watch on her until she wakes up. She is in a coma."

"When will she come out of the coma?" her mother asked.

"That is not certain. Her body is trying to heal itself and the coma keeps her inert so that can happen. But with all the injuries that she has and others that we don't know about, that may take a long time."

Hope began to cry and hug her parents. "I can't believe this happened. Why did this have to happen to her? I would rather be there in that bed instead."

"Oh, Hope. Don't say such things. This was an accident. A terrible accident that shouldn't have happened if she had been wearing a seatbelt."

"Dear, you can't blame her friend's mother. She thought Esme had it on," her husband said as he placed his arm around her shoulders to steady her.

The nurse announced that they had to leave now to take Esme for more x-rays. "You can wait in the waiting room and someone will get you when she is brought back here. We are waiting for a room for her. That should be shortly."

Esme's parents and sister nodded and turned to leave but were stopped by the nurse. "I know how difficult this is for you. She is your baby. Something happened to my child like this, too, years ago. All you can do is pray. That is what I did. HE will give you support and strength."

"Thank you, nurse. We plan to do plenty of that."

When they got back into the waiting room the mother of Esme's friend was there with her husband. She jumped up to hug them but was pushed away by Esme's mother.

"I can't talk to you now. I am upset. I don't understand how this could have happened. You didn't take care of my daughter."

"I know. I'm so sorry. If I had known that Esme did not have her seatbelt on, I wouldn't have driven away. We were hit by a teen that had been drinking. His alcohol level was off the charts. It was a terrible accident. I wish it never happened."

"Yes, it was. We need to pray for her now. Esme needs all the prayers that we can give her. HE will help us."

"Yes. Please let me sit here with you and pray."

They all sat and prayed silently as they waited for someone to come out to let them know how this little girl was doing.

Hope was praying not only for her sister's recovery but also for her baby. She had to share this news with her parents but didn't know how to do that now with what had happened to her sister. She didn't know if they could take any more shocks.

Her mother looked at her and inquired, "Are you all right, Hope. You look like you are going to be sick."

"I don't feel very good, Mom. I have an upset stomach and think I might be sick."

"Oh, sweetheart, let's take you to the ladies' room. Your father will be here when the nurse comes out to see us."

Her mother escorted her to the bathroom and waited outside the stall as her daughter was sick. "Do you feel better now, honey?"

"A little bit, Mom. Thanks. I am a little hungry now. I haven't eaten much today. Can I get a snack and a drink?"

"Sure. Let's go back and see your father first. They may have brought Esme back from her tests."

Hope bent over and gasped. I need to go back to the bathroom, Mom. I'm sorry," she said as she hurried back to the bathroom just in time.

Her mother followed her again and waited for her to finish.

"Are you sure you are okay, Hope?"

"I'm…well…I have to tell you something, Mom. I'm so sorry. I didn't mean for it to happen."

"What are you saying, Hope? Are you pregnant?"

"Yes, I am. Oh, Mom, please forgive me! He said he loved me. I thought that we would be together. I never expected to get pregnant the first time."

"That can happen, Hope. We will deal with this. First, we must see your sister through this horrific accident. I will tell your father when it is the right time. Right now, he is too distraught and can't handle another shock. Go get some crackers and ginger ale. That may help settle your stomach for now."

"Okay, Mom. Thanks for understanding. I…didn't know how I was going to tell you."

Her mother nodded, "Hurry back. I will be with your father."

Hope's mother had received another unexpected shock. She couldn't believe what was happening to their family. They were growing and at the same time possibly losing one member. She said another prayer for HIM to keep her youngest daughter safe. She couldn't handle losing her.

The nurse was talking to her husband when she got back to the waiting room. "Is she doing better? Do you know anymore?"

"No, I'm afraid not. We will set her broken bones and keep her on an IV and monitor her closely. She is still able to breathe on her own. You can come in to see her. We cleaned her up a little from her head wound."

"Thank you. It was frightening to see her with all that blood on her face. Do you think she will wake up soon?"

"We don't know that as the doctor told you. It is a wait and see if the body can heal on its own. Talk to her. That helps both of you. She needs to know that you are here and encourage her to come back to you."

"Will she be able to hear us?" the father asked.

"We think so but no one really knows that. Only she will know that you care. When she does wake up, ask her if she heard you."

"Did your child hear you?" the mother asked.

"I hope she did. I would like to think so." The nurse turned abruptly and left the room before they could ask her anything more.

Hope hurried back from the cafeteria with a tray containing a ginger ale, a package of crackers, and coffees for her parents and the other mother and father.

"Thank you, Hope. I could use some caffeine about now. We just spoke with the nurse. We are going in to see your sister," her mother explained.

"Did she wake up, Mom?"

"No, but the nurse suggested that we talk to her and let her know we love her and want her to wake up."

"Can she hear us in a coma?" Hope inquired.

"I don't know. I guess no one knows that for sure. But we have to try and not give up on her. Esme is in there and she will hear us. Let's try and tell her that we are praying for her too."

"Of course, Mom. I've been praying every minute since I knew about the accident."

"That's good, Hope. Keep praying. HE will help us."

They stayed with Esme for as long as they could and after she was moved into a room in the ICU. They had to leave when a nurse came to tell them visiting hours were over.

"I can't leave my baby!" the father exclaimed.

"You can come back tomorrow. Your daughter will be in good hands. She has the best doctor in the business and I will be on call with her tonight. I promise to watch over her like she was my own daughter," the nurse explained.

The mother asked, "Is your daughter all recovered now since her accident?"

The nurse shook her head. "My daughter died a month after being in a coma. She never regained consciousness from a brain injury."

Esme's mother caught her breath and said, "Oh my goodness. I am so sorry. I didn't mean to pry."

"No, that's okay. It was a few years ago and I am still in shock over her death but I knew that she would never have been the same if she did come out of the coma. She would have lived in a facility forever without being able to talk, walk, see, or eat. It was a blessing. At the time I didn't feel that way, but now I know better."

"Oh, I see. Will my daughter be a vegetable if she wakes up?"

"We don't know that. I'm sorry I shared that with you. Each case is different. Your daughter will wake up and be fine. It may take a while, that is all."

"Oh, okay. Thank you."

"Please go home and eat something. You must be strong for her. She will need you in the days to come. Take care and pray."

"We will. Thank you again. God bless you."

"And you too."

Hope followed her parents out to the lobby where they met the other parents. "Please go home. We won't know anything more now. Esme is in the ICU and will be monitored. They will call us if there is any change. Thank you for your support and forgive me for blaming you for this accident."

"That's okay. I feel somewhat responsible. We will keep praying and talk to you tomorrow. Please let us know if there is any change before then."

"Yes, we will. Thank you," Esme's mother said.

CHAPTER 2

Each day the family visited with Esme, sat by her side, and spoke to her. They shared that they would celebrate her birthday once she woke up. They had presents to give her and wanted her to enjoy them. They urged her to wake up so she could.

After a month in the coma Esme still had not stirred. Hope sat there watching her while their parents walked out to use the facilities and grab a coffee and sandwich and something for Hope.

She thought it was time to share her news with her sister. Her father had accepted it but was still shocked over the idea of having a new baby in the house and being a grandfather.

Hope took Esme's hand in hers and spoke softly. "Esme, I have news for you. You need to wake up in order to be an auntie. I am going to have a baby in seven months. I want my baby to know you and how sweet and kind you are. She needs you, Esme. I need you. Please wake up!"

Tears filled Hope's eyes as she watched her sister's face and stroked her hand. She suddenly felt a finger beneath her hand move ever so little, but enough to know that it was Esme doing it.

"Esme, are you there? Please do that again! Move your fingers, Esme. I want to feel that again. I know you can do it!"

Their parents came into the room with their food and stopped short when they heard Hope's words.

"Did she move her hand, Hope?" her mother asked.

"Yes, Mom. She did! I am trying to get her to do it again. I told her about the baby. I think she wants to wake up and be an auntie. I told her my baby needs her and so do I."

"Oh, Hope. Try that again. Remind her that the baby will need her," her mother explained.

Hope kept repeating, "Esme, please wake up. I need you to be an auntie to my baby. She or he will need you. I don't know whether it is a boy or girl but will find out soon. Please come back to us!"

The nurse came into the room at this moment to check on Esme and heard Hope's pleading words.

"Did she move?"

"Yes, nurse. I felt her finger move under my hand. I know she heard me when I urged her to wake up."

"Good. That is a good sign that she is coming out of the coma slowly. It may take another day or more for her to completely wake up."

"How long will it be for her to completely recover from the coma once she wakes up?" the father asked.

"That is difficult to say. It is different in every case. We will keep watching her for any signs that she is lucid. She may have to stay here for another month or more until she can walk, talk, eat and do all the necessary things to begin anew."

"Will she remember what happened?" her mother asked.

"Time will tell. Her memory may take a while to come back. We can't push her too much to remember. We will let her remember on her own. Okay?"

"Okay" they all agreed.

"I will let the doctor know of her latest move. He may come in soon to speak with you."

"Thank you, nurse," they said in unison.

Hope hugged her parents and squeezed her sister's hand at the same time to keep the connection. She felt her sister's finger move again but this time all of them moved under her hand.

"Esme, wake up!" Hope cried.

They watched and waited for Esme to make another move.

Esme moved her hand and squeezed her sister's hand back lightly.

"She squeezed my hand, Mom and Dad! She did it! She's coming back!"

The parents gathered closer and held onto Esme's other hand waiting to feel her squeeze their hands.

They cried out in relief when she did and shed happy tears as they kissed her hand and held on tight.

The doctor came into the room at that moment and went to Esme's side to check her eyes for any sign that she was responding.

When he did, Esme's eyes opened on their own and she smiled at him and at her parents and sister.

"Esme! You are back!" her family announced, in jubilation.

The doctor checked Esme over and nodded to her parents. "She has come back! Now it is time to work to get her back completely. She will have a road to travel yet but the worst is over. Thank God."

"Yes, Thanks to God! HE brought her back!" her parents declared through happy tears.

Esme squeezed her sister's hand again and smiled.

"I guess you really want to be an auntie, huh, Esme?" Hope asked her as her tears flowed in relief.

She had her sister back and was thankful that her baby who, in her or his own way, brought her sister back. It was like having two miracles in one.

THE END

ABOUT THE AUTHOR

J.E. Spina is a retired administrative secretary from a public school system in Massachusetts. She has always loved writing poetry, novels and children's stories. She published her first book in 2013 and hasn't stopped since.

This is the 50th book J.E. aka Janice Spina has published. She has published nine other novels and another short story collection for 18+ under J.E. Spina.

She also writes under Janice Spina and has two mystery series of six books each, one for boys and the other for girls which is enjoyed by both boys and girls, a fantasy series for young adults and twenty-three stories for young children.

She can be reached at these links.

Website: https://Jemsbooks.com
Blog: https://Jemsbooks.blog
Twitter: https://twitter.com/janice_spina
FB Main Page: https://facebook.com/janice.spina.9
FB Author Page: https://facebook.com/janicespina7
FB Novelist Page: https://facebook.com/jespina7

J.E. lives in New Hampshire with her husband, John, and a tank of tropical fish. John is the illustrator of her children's books and designer of all her book covers.

If you enjoyed this book, please leave a review where you purchased it and spread the word to your family and friends. J.E. loves to hear from readers and welcomes reviews from wherever her books are purchased. She says, 'It's like Christmas each time I receive a review!'

If you would like to be on Janice Spina' aka J.E. Spina's email list to receive updates, newsletters, and special deals on books, please follow her blog at link above.

Watch for more books coming from JemsBooks.

A NOTE FROM THE AUTHOR

This is the second short story collection I have written in eclectic genres. There are six stories for you to enjoy. I find it fascinating to create short stories for all ages and plan to create more in the near future.

I hope you enjoyed this work of fiction. Watch for more books coming over the next year or so.

Thank you for purchasing one of Jemsbooks. I appreciate your kind support of me and my books. If you like this book, a review would be greatly appreciated wherever you purchased it. Reviews and word of mouth are the best way to spread your thoughts about books. Please share your review with friends and family. I would love to hear from you. You can reach me at jjspina@comcast.net.

All my books are available on Amazon and Barnes & Noble. Watch for more books coming for all ages.

With Blessings & Love,

Janice Spina

YA BOOKS BY JANICE SPINA - PG 13+

The Legend of the Taken Ones (Gateskin Chronicles Book 1)
Mom's Choice Awards – Gold Medal
Book Excellence Award Finalist

The Unknown Territory (Gateskin Chronicles Book 2)
Mom's Choice Awards – Gold Medal
Maincrest Media Book Awards

Search for the Medallion (Gateskin Chronicles Book 3)
Mom's Choice Awards – Gold Medal

More books coming in the next year and beyond!

OTHER MG/PT/YA BOOKS BY JANICE SPINA - 10+

Davey & Derek Junior Detectives Book 1: The Case of the Missing Cell Phone
Pinnacle Book Achievement Award
Honorable Mention- Readers' Favorite Book Award

Davey & Derek Junior Detectives Book 2: The Case of the Mysterious Black Cat
Pinnacle Book Achievement Award

Davey & Derek Junior Detectives Book 3: The Case of the Magical Ivory Elephant
Pinnacle Book Achievement Award
Reader's Favorite Book Awards – Silver Medal

Davey & Derek Junior Detectives Book 4: The Case of the Brown Scraggly Dog
Top Shelf Book Awards – First Place
Finalist in Red City Review Awards
5-Star Book Review – Readers' Favorite Book Awards

Davey & Derek Junior Detectives Book 5: The Case of the Sad Mischievous Ghost
Pinnacle Book Achievement Award

Authorsdb Cover Contest – Silver Medal

Davey & Derek Junior Detectives Book 6: The Case of the Mystery of the Bells
Pinnacle Book Achievement Award
Finalist – Readers' Favorite Book Awards
Finalist – Book Excellence Awards

Abby & Holly School Dance
Pinnacle Book Achievement Award
Readers' Favorite Book Awards – Bronze Medal

Abby & Holly Series Book 2: Unfortunate Events
Pinnacle Book Achievement Award
Readers' Favorite Book Awards – Honorable Mention

Abby & Holly Series, Book 3, Secrets of the Trunk
Pinnacle Book Achievement Award

Abby & Holly Series, Book 4, The Hidden Stairway
Pinnacle Book Achievement Award

Abby & Holly Series, Book 5, The Copper Key
Pinnacle Book Achievement Award

Abby & Holly Series, Book 6, Faulty Timeline
Pinnacle Book Achievement Award

More MG/PT books coming over the next few years!

BOOKS BY J.E. SPINA FOR 15+

The Misunderstood Angel (Branyrd the Angel Series Book 1)
Five-Star review from Readers' Favorite Book Awards

Mission of Mercy (Branyrd the Angel Series Book 2)

Mission of Love (Branyrd the Angel Series Book 3)

Mission of Hope (Branyrd the Angel Series Book 4)

BOOKS BY J.E. SPINA FOR 18+

Hunting Mariah
Finalist in Authorsdb First Lines Contest
Maincrest Media Book Award

Mariah's Revenge
Finalist in Authorsdb First Lines Contest

How Far is Heaven
Five-Star review from Readers' Favorite Book
Awards

***An Angel Among Us: A Short Story Collection
In A Second***
Five-Star review from Readers' Favorite Book
Awards

Lubelia Alycea: One Hundred Years
Five-Star review from Readers' Favorite Book
Awards

www.ingramcontent.com/pod-product-compliance
Lightning Source LLC
Chambersburg PA
CBHW051312170626
46809CB00004B/1857

* 9 7 9 8 9 8 7 4 6 4 6 7 0 *